In
1935 if you wanted to
read a good book, you needed
either a lot of money or a library card.
Cheap paperbacks were available, but their
poor production generally mirrored the quality
between the covers. One weekend that year,
Allen Lane, Managing Director of The Bodley Head,
having spent the weekend visiting Agatha Christie,
found himself on a platform at Exeter station trying to
find something to read for his journey back to London.
He was appalled by the quality of the material he had to
choose from. Everything that Allen Lane achieved from that
day until his death in 1970 was based on a passionate belief
in the existence of 'a vast reading public for *intelligent*
books at a low price'. The result of his momentous vision
was the birth not only of Penguin, but of the 'paperback
revolution'. Quality writing became available for the price of
a packet of cigarettes, literature became a mass medium
for the first time, a nation of book-borrowers became a
nation of book-buyers – and the very concept of book
publishing was changed for ever. Those founding
principles – of quality and value, with an overarching
belief in the fundamental importance of reading –
have guided everything the company has
done since 1935. Sir Allen Lane's
pioneering spirit is still very much alive
at Penguin in 2005. Here's to
the next 70 years!

MORE THAN A BUSINESS

'We decided it was time to end the almost customary half-hearted manner in which cheap editions were produced – as though the only people who could possibly want cheap editions must belong to a lower order of intelligence. We, however, believed in the existence in this country of a vast reading public for intelligent books at a low price, and staked everything on it'
Sir Allen Lane, 1902–1970

'The Penguin Books are splendid value for sixpence, so splendid that if other publishers had any sense they would combine against them and suppress them'
George Orwell

'More than a business … a national cultural asset'
Guardian

'When you look at the whole Penguin achievement you know that it constitutes, in action, one of the more democratic successes of our recent social history'
Richard Hoggart

The Snobs

MURIEL SPARK

PENGUIN BOOKS

Published by the Penguin Group
Penguin Books Ltd, 80 Strand, London WC2R ORL, England
Penguin Group (USA) Inc., 375 Hudson Street, New York, New York 10014, USA
Penguin Group (Canada), 10 Alcorn Avenue, Toronto, Ontario, Canada M4V 3B2
(a division of Pearson Penguin Canada Inc.)
Penguin Ireland, 25 St Stephen's Green, Dublin 2, Ireland
(a division of Penguin Books Ltd)
Penguin Group (Australia), 250 Camberwell Road, Camberwell, Victoria 3124,
Australia (a division of Pearson Australia Group Pty Ltd)
Penguin Books India Pvt Ltd, 11 Community Centre,
Panchsheel Park, New Delhi – 110 017, India
Penguin Group (NZ), cnr Airborne and Rosedale Roads, Albany,
Auckland 1310, New Zealand (a division of Pearson New Zealand Ltd)
Penguin Books (South Africa) (Pty) Ltd, 24 Sturdee Avenue,
Rosebank 2196, South Africa

Penguin Books Ltd, Registered Offices: 80 Strand, London WC2R ORL, England

www.penguin.com

The Complete Short Stories published by Viking 2001
Published in Penguin Books 2002
This extract published as a Pocket Penguin 2005

1

Set in 11/13pt Monotype Dante
Typeset by Palimpsest Book Production Limited
Polmont, Stirlingshire
Printed in England by Clays Ltd, St Ives plc

Contents

The Snobs

Snob: A person who sets too much value on social standing, wishing to be associated with the upper class and their mores, and treating those viewed as inferior with condescension and contempt' – *Chambers Dictionary*.

I feel bound to quote the above definition, it so well fits the Ringer-Smith couple whom I knew in the nineteen-fifties and of whom I have since met variations and versions enough to fill me with wonder. Snobs are really amazing. They mainly err in failing to fool the very set of people they are hoping to be accepted by, and above all, to seem to belong to, to be taken for. They may live in a democratic society – it does nothing to help. Nothing.

Of the Ringer-Smith couple, he, Jake, was the more snobbish. She, at least, had a certain natural serenity of behaviour which she herself never questioned. She was in fact rather smug. Her background was of small land-owning farmers and minor civil servants. She, Marion, was stingy, stingy as hell. Jake also had a civil service background and, on the mother's side, a family of fruit export-import affairs which had not left her very well off, the inheritance having been absorbed by the male members of the family. Jake and Marion were a fairly suitable match. He was slightly the shorter of the two. Both were skinny. They had no children. Skeletons in the family cupboard do nothing to daunt the true snob, in fact they provoke a certain arrogance, and this was the case with Jake. A family scandal on a national scale had grown to an international one. A spectacular bank robbery with murder on the part of a brother had resulted in the family name being reduced to a byword in every household. The delinquent Ringer-Smith and his associates had escaped to a safe exile in South America leaving Jake and his ageing mother to face the music of the press and TV reporters. Nobody would have taken it out on them in the normal way if it had not been for the contempt with which they treated police, journalists, interrogators, functionaries of the law and the public in general. They put on airs suggesting that they were untouchably 'good family', and they generally carried on as if they were earls and marquises instead of ordinary middle-class people. No earl, no marquis at present alive would in fact be so haughty unless he were completely out of his mind or perhaps an unfortunate drug addict or losing gambler.

I was staying with some friends at a château near Dijon when the Ringer-Smiths turned up. This was in the nineties. I hardly recognized them. The Ringer-Smiths had not just turned up at the château, they were found by Anne, bewildered, outside the village shop, puzzling over a map, uncertain of their way to any-where. Warming towards their plight as she always would towards those in trouble, Anne invited these lost English people for a cup of tea at the château where they could work out their route.

Anne and Monty, English themselves, had lived in the château for the last eight years. It was a totally unex-pected inheritance from the last member of a distant

branch of Monty's family. The house and small fo.
that went with it came to him in his early fifties a.
enormous surprise. He had been a shoe salesman a
a bus driver, among other things. Anne had been a stoc
broker's secretary. Their two children, both girls, were
married and away. The 'fairy tale' story of their inheritance was in the newspapers for a day, but it wasn't
everybody who read the passing news.

Monty was out when Anne brought home the Ringer-
Smiths. I was watching the television – some programme which now escapes me for ever due to the shock
of seeing those people. Anne, tall, merry, blonded-up
and carrying her sixties well, took herself off to the
kitchen to put on the kettle. She had made the sitting-
room as much like England as possible.

'Who does this place belong to?' Jake inquired of me
as soon as Anne was out of the room. Obviously, he
had not recognized me in the present context, although
I felt Marion's eyes upon me in a penetrating stare of
puzzlement, of quasi-remembrance

'It belongs,' I said, 'to the lady who invited you to
tea.'

'Oh!' he said

'Haven't we met?' Marion was speaking to me.

'Yes, you have.' I made myself known.

'What brings you here?' said Jake outright.

'The same as brings you here. I was invited.'

Anne returned with the tea, served with a silver te
service and pretty china cups. She carried the followed
a young girl who was helping in th
with hot water and a plate of '

u speak English very well,' Jake said.

Oh, we are English,' said Anne. 'But we live in France w. My husband inherited the château from his family n his mother's side, the Martineaus.'

'Oh, of course,' said Jake.

The factor came in from the farm and took a cup of tea standing up. He addressed Anne as 'Madame'.

Anne was already regretting her impulse in asking the couple to tea. They said very little but just sat on. She was afraid they would miss the last bus to the station. Looking at me, she said, 'The last bus goes at six, doesn't it?'

I said to Marion, 'You don't want to miss the last bus.'

'Could we see round the château?' said Marion. 'The guidebook says it's fourteenth century.'

'Well, not all of it is,' said Anne. 'But today is a bit difficult. We don't, you know, open the house to the public. We live in it.'

'I'm sure we've met,' said Marion to Anne, as if this took care of their catching the last bus – a point which was not lost on Anne. Kindly though she was I knew she hated to have to ferry people by car to the station and take on other chores she was not prepared for. I could see, already in Anne's mind, the thought: 'I have to get rid of these people or they'll stay for dinner and then all night. They are château-grabbers.'

Anne had often lamented to me about the château-grabbers of her later life. People who didn't want to know her when she was obscure and a bus driver's wife much wanted to know her intimately. Monty didn't care of organ this, one way or another. But then the work als and entertaining in style fell more

on Anne than on Monty, who mostly spent his t
helping the factor in the grounds, game-keeping a
forest-clearing.

Anne could see that the English couple she had
invited in 'for a cup of tea' were clingers, climbers,
general nuisances, and she especially cast a look of
desperation at me when Marion Ringer-Smith said, 'I'm
sure we've met.'

'You think so?' Anne said. She had got up and was
leading the way to the back door. 'This is the *Cour des
Adieus*,' she said; 'it leads quicker to your bus stop.'
Marion stooped and took a cake as if it was her last
chance of ever eating a cake again.

I was at this moment coming to the end of a novel
I was writing. Anne had offered me the peace and quiet
of French château life and the informality of her own
life-style which made it an ideal arrangement. She had
also undertaken to type out the novel from any hand-
written manuscripts on to a word-processor. But now
at a quarter to six, I could see the rest of our afternoon's
plans slipping away.

I doubted that Marion had indeed seen Anne before.
It was by some mental process of transference that
she had picked on Anne. The one she had actually met
was myself, but she wasn't very much aware of it.
After a gap of forty years, she remembered very little
of me.

Jake Ringer-Smith asked if he could use the bathroom. Oh, you bore, I thought. Why don't you go? There
are trees and thick bushes all the way down the bath-
for you to pee on. But no, he had to be us time. Jake
room. It was nearly ten minu

ed his backpack over to his wife and said, 'Take this,
will you?'

'I would really like to see round the château,' Marion
said, 'while we're here and since we've come all this
way.'

I had come across this situation before. There are
people who will hold up a party of tired and worn fellow
travellers just because *they* have to see a pulpit. There
are people who will arrive an hour late for dinner with
the excuse that they had to see over some art gallery on
the way. Marion was very much one of those. If chal-
lenged she would have thought nothing of pointing out
that, after all, she had paid a plane fare to arrive at where
she was. I remember Marion's shapeless cheesecloth
dress and her worn sandals and Jake's baggy, ostenta-
tiously patched, grubby trousers, their avidity to get on
intimate terms with the lady of the house, to be invited
to supper and, no doubt, to spend the night. I was really
sorry for Anne who, I was aware, was sorry for herself
and most of all regretting her own impulsive invitation
to a cup of tea in her house.

Anne kept a soup kitchen in a building some way
from the house, beyond a vegetable garden. She was
pledged, I knew, to be there and help whenever possible, at six-thirty every evening. Laboriously, she
explained this to the Ringer-Smiths. '. . . otherwise I'd
have been glad to show you the house, not that there's
much to see.'

'Soup kitchen!' said Jake. 'May we join it for a bowl
of soup? Then perhaps we can stretch out our sleeping-
bags and see the night under one of your charming archways
here tomorrow.'

Does this sound like a nightmare? It was a nightmare. Nothing could throw off these people.

Down at the soup kitchen that evening, dispensing slabs of bread and cheese with bowls of tomato soup, I was not surprised to see the Ringer-Smiths appear.

'We belong to the lower orders,' he said to me with an exaggeratedly self-effacing grin that meant 'We do not belong to any lower orders and just see how grand we really are – *we* don't care what we look like or what company we keep. We are Us.'

In fact they looked positively shifty among the genuine skin-and-bone tramps and hairy drop-outs and bulging bag-ladies. I dished out their portions to them without a smile. They had missed the last bus. Somehow, Anne and Monty had to arrange for them to have a bedroom for the night. 'We stayed at the Château Leclaire de Martineau at Dijon' I could hear them telling their friends.

Before breakfast I advised Anne and Monty to make themselves scarce. 'Otherwise,' I said, 'you'll never get rid of them. Leave them to me.'

'I'm sure,' said Marion, 'I've met Anne before. But I can't tell where.'

'She has been a cook in many houses,' I said. 'And Monty has been a butler.'

'A cook and a butler?' said Jake.

'Yes, the master and mistress are away from home at present.'

'But she *told me she was the owner*,' Marion said, indicating the dining-room door with her head.

'Oh no, you must be mistaken.'

'But I'm sure she said –'

'Not at all,' I said. 'What a pity you can't see over the château. Such lovely pictures. But the Comtesse will be here at any moment. I don't know how you will explain yourselves. So far as I know you haven't been invited.'

'Oh we have,' said Jake. 'The servants begged us to stay. So typical, posing as the lord and lady of the manor! But it's getting late, we'll miss the bus.'

They were off within four minutes, tramping down the drive with their bulging packs.

Anne and Monty were delighted when I told them how it was done. Anne was sure, judging from a previous experience, that the intruders had planned to stay for a week.

'What else can you do with people like that?' said Anne.

'Put them in a story if you are me,' I said. 'And sell the story.'

'Can they sue?'

'Let them sue,' I said. 'Let them go ahead, stand up, and say Yes, that was Us.'

'An eccentric couple. They took the soap with them,' said Anne.

Monty went off about his business with a smile. So did Anne. And I, too. Or so I thought.

It was eleven-thirty, two hours later that morning, when, looking out of the window of my room as I often do when I am working on a novel, I saw them again under one of the trees bordering a lawn. They were looking up towards the house.

I had no idea where Monty and Anne were at that moment, nor could I think how to locate the factor,

Raoul, or his wife, Marie-Louise. This was a disturbance in the rhythm of my morning's work, but I decided to go down and see what was the matter. As soon as they saw me Marion said, 'Oh hallo. We decided it was uncivil of us to leave without seeing the lady of the house and paying our respects.'

'We'll wait till the Comtesse arrives,' Jake stated.

'Well, you're unlucky,' I said. 'I believe there's word come through that she'll be away for a week.'

'That's all right,' said Marion. 'We can spare a week.'

'Only civil . . .' said Jake.

I managed to alert Anne before she saw them. They were very cool to her when she did at last appear before them. 'The Comtesse would, I'm sure, be offended if we left without a word of thanks,' said Jake.

'Not at all,' said Anne. 'In fact, you *have to go*.'

'Not so,' said Marion.

Raoul tackled them, joined by Monty. Marion had already reclaimed their bedroom. 'As the beds had to be changed anyway,' she said, 'we may as well stay on. We don't mind eating down at the shed.' By this she meant the soup kitchen. 'We are not above eating with the proletariat,' said Jake.

Raoul and I searched the house, every drawer, for a key to the door of their bedroom. Eventually we found one that fitted and succeeded in locking them out. Monty took their packs and dumped them outside the gates of the château. These operations took place while they were feeding in the soup kitchen. We all five (Marie-Louise had joined us) confronted them and told them what we had done.

What happened to them after that none of us quite

knows. We do know that they went to retrieve their bags and found themselves locked out by the factor. Anne received a letter, correctly addressed to her as the Comtesse, from Jake, indignantly complaining about the treatment they had received at the hands of the 'staff.'

'Something,' wrote Jake, 'told me not to accept their invitation. I knew instinctively that they were not one of us. I should have listened to my instincts. People like them are such frightful snobs.'

The First Year of My Life

I was born on the first day of the second month of the last year of the First World War, a Friday. Testimony abounds that during the first year of my life I never smiled. I was known as the baby whom nothing and no one could make smile. Everyone who knew me then has told me so. They tried very hard, singing and bouncing me up and down, jumping around, pulling faces. Many times I was told this later by my family and their friends; but, anyway, I knew it at the time.

You will shortly be hearing of that new school of psychology, or maybe you have heard of it already, which after long and far-adventuring research and experiment has established that all of the young of the human species are born omniscient. Babies, in their waking hours, know everything that is going on everywhere in the world; they can tune in to any conversation they choose, switch on to any scene. We have all experienced this power. It is only after the first year that it was brainwashed out of us; for it is demanded of us by our immediate environment that we grow to be of use to it in a practical way. Gradually, our know-all brain-cells are blacked out although traces remain in some individuals in the form of ESP, and in the adults of some primitive tribes.

It is not a new theory. Poets and philosophers, as usual, have been there first. But scientific proof is now ready and to hand. Perhaps the final touches are being put to the new manifesto in some cell at Harvard University. Any day now it will be given to the world, and the world will be convinced.

Let me therefore get my word in first, because I feel pretty sure, now, about the authenticity of my remembrance of things past. My autobiography, as I very well perceived at the time, started in the very worst year that the world had ever seen so far. Apart from being born bedridden and toothless, unable to raise myself on the pillow or utter anything but farmyard squawks or police-siren wails, my bladder and my bowels totally out of control, I was further depressed by the curious behaviour of the two-legged mammals around me. There were those black-dressed people, females of the species to which I appeared to belong, saying they had lost their sons. I slept a great deal. Let them go and find their sons. It was like the special pin for my nappies which my mother or some other hoverer dedicated to my care was always losing. These careless women in black lost their husbands and their brothers. Then they came to visit my mother and clucked and crowed over my cradle. I was not amused.

'Babies never really smile till they're three months old,' said my mother. 'They're not *supposed* to smile till they're three months old.'

My brother, aged six, marched up and down with a toy rifle over his shoulder:

> The grand old Duke of York
> He had ten thousand men;
> He marched them up to the top of the hill
> And he marched them down again.

And when they were up, they were up.
And when they were down, they were down.
And when they were neither down nor up
They were neither up nor down.

'Just listen to him!'
'Look at him with his rifle!'
I was about ten days old when Russia stopped
fighting. I tuned in to the Czar, a prisoner, with the rest
of his family, since evidently the country had put him
off his throne and there had been a revolution not long
before I was born. Everyone was talking about it. I tuned
in to the Czar. 'Nothing would ever induce me to sign
the treaty of Brest-Litovsk,' he said to his wife. Anyway,
nobody had asked him to.

At this point I was sleeping twenty hours a day to
get my strength up. And from what I discerned in the
other four hours of the day I knew I was going to need
it. The Western Front on my frequency was sheer blood,
mud, dismembered bodies, blistered crashes, hectic
flashes of light in the night skies, explosions, total terror.
Since it was plain I had been born into a bad moment
in the history of the world, the future bothered me,
unable as I was to raise my head from the pillow and
as yet only twenty inches long. 'I truly wish I were a
fox or a bird,' D. H. Lawrence was writing to somebody.
Dreary old creeping Jesus. I fell asleep.

Red sheets of flame shot across the sky. It was 21st
March, the fiftieth day of my life, and the German
Spring Offensive had started before my morning feed.
Infinite slaughter. I scowled at the scene, and made an
effort to kick out. But the attempt was feeble. Furious,

and impatient for some strength, I wailed for my feed.
After which I stopped wailing but continued to scowl.

> The grand old Duke of York
> He had ten thousand men . . .

They rocked the cradle. I never heard a sillier song. Over
in Berlin and Vienna the people were starving, freezing,
striking, rioting and yelling in the streets. In London
everyone was bustling to work and muttering that it
was time the whole damn business was over.

The big people around me bared their teeth; that
meant a smile, it meant they were pleased or amused.
They spoke of ration cards for meat and sugar and
butter.

'Where will it all end?'

I went to sleep. I woke and tuned in to Bernard Shaw
who was telling someone to shut up. I switched over to
Joseph Conrad who, strangely enough, was saying precisely the same thing. I still didn't think it worth a smile,
although it was expected of me any day now. I got on to
Turkey. Women draped in black huddled and chattered
in their harems; yak-yak-yak. This was boring, so I came
back to home base.

In and out came and went the women in British black.
My mother's brother, dressed in his uniform, came
coughing. He had been poison-gassed in the trenches.
'Tout le monde à la bataille!' declaimed Marshal Foch the
old swine. He was now Commander-in-Chief of the
Allied Forces. My uncle coughed from deep within his
lungs, never to recover but destined to return to the
Front. His brass buttons gleamed in the firelight. I

weighed twelve pounds by now; I stretched and kicked for exercise, seeing that I had a lifetime before me, coping with this crowd. I took six feeds a day and kept most of them down by the time the *Vindictive* was sunk in Ostend harbour, on which day I kicked with special vigour in my bath.

In France the conscripted soldiers leapfrogged over the dead on the advance and littered the fields with limbs and hands, or drowned in the mud. The strongest men on all fronts were dead before I was born. Now the sentries used bodies for barricades and the fighting men were unhealthy from the start. I checked my toes and fingers, knowing I was going to need them. *The Playboy of the Western World* was playing at the Court Theatre in London, but occasionally I beamed over to the House of Commons which made me drop off gently to sleep. Generally, I preferred the Western Front where one got the true state of affairs. It was essential to know the worst, blood and explosions and all, for one had to be prepared, as the boy scouts said. Virginia Woolf yawned and reached for her diary. Really, I preferred the Western Front.

In the fifth month of my life I could raise my head from my pillow and hold it up. I could grasp the objects that were held out to me. Some of these things rattled and squawked. I gnawed on them to get my teeth started. 'She hasn't smiled yet?' said the dreary old aunties. My mother, on the defensive, said I was probably one of those late smilers. On my wavelength Pablo Picasso was getting married and early in that month of July the Silver Wedding of King George V and Queen Mary was celebrated in joyous pomp at St Paul's

Cathedral. They drove through the streets of London with their children. Twenty-five years of domestic happiness. A lot of fuss and ceremonial handing over of swords went on at the Guildhall where the King and Queen received a cheque for £53,000 to dispose of for charity as they thought fit. *Tout le monde à la bataille!* Income tax in England had reached six shillings in the pound. Everyone was talking about the Silver Wedding; yak-yak-yak, and ten days later the Czar and his family, now in Siberia, were invited to descend to a little room in the basement. Crack, crack, went the guns; screams and blood all over the place, and that was the end of the Romanoffs. I flexed my muscles. 'A fine healthy baby,' said the doctor; which gave me much satisfaction.

Tout le monde à la bataille! That included my gassed uncle. My health had improved to the point where I was able to crawl in my playpen. Bertrand Russell was still cheerily in prison for writing something seditious about pacifism. Tuning in as usual to the Front Lines it looked as if the Germans were winning all the battles yet losing the war. And so it was. The upper-income people were upset about the income tax at six shillings to the pound. But all women over thirty got the vote. 'It seems a long time to wait,' said one of my drab old aunts, aged twenty-two. The speeches in the House of Commons always sent me to sleep which was why I missed, at the actual time, a certain oration by Mr Asquith following the armistice on 11th November. Mr Asquith was a greatly esteemed former prime minister later to be an Earl, and had been ousted by Mr Lloyd George. I clearly heard Asquith, in private, refer to Lloyd George as 'that damned Welsh goat'.

The armistice was signed and I was awake for that. I pulled myself on to my feet with the aid of the bars of my cot. My teeth were coming through very nicely in my opinion, and well worth all the trouble I was put to in bringing them forth. I weighed twenty pounds. On all the world's fighting fronts the men killed in action or dead of wounds numbered 8,538,315 and the warriors wounded and maimed were 21,219,452. With these figures in mind I sat up in my high chair and banged my spoon on the table. One of my mother's black-draped friends recited:

> I have a rendezvous with Death
> At some disputed barricade,
> When spring comes back with rustling shade
> And apple blossoms fill the air –
> I have a rendezvous with Death.

Most of the poets, they said, had been killed. The poetry made them dab their eyes with clean white hand kerchiefs.

Next February on my first birthday, there was a birthday cake with one candle. Lots of children and their elders. The war had been over two months and twenty-one days. 'Why doesn't she smile?' My brother was to blow out the candle. The elders were talking about the war and the political situation. Lloyd George and Asquith, Asquith and Lloyd George. I remembered recently having switched on to Mr Asquith at a private party where he had been drinking a lot. He was playing cards and when he came to cut the cards he tried to cut a large box of matches by mistake. On another occasion I had seen him putting his arm around a lady's shoulder in a Daimler motor car, and generally behaving towards her in a very friendly fashion. Strangely enough she said, 'If you don't stop this nonsense immediately I'll order the chauffeur to stop and I'll get out.' Mr Asquith replied, 'And pray, what reason will you give?' Well anyway it was my feeding time.

The guests arrived for my birthday. It was so sad, said one of the black widows, so sad about Wilfred Owen who was killed so late in the war, and she quoted from a poem of his:

> What passing-bells for these who die as cattle?
> Only the monstrous anger of the guns.

The children were squealing and toddling around. One was sick and another wet the floor and stood with his legs apart gaping at the puddle. All was mopped up. I banged my spoon on the table of my high chair.

> But I've a rendezvous with Death
> At midnight in some flaming town;
> When spring trips north again this year,
> And I to my pledged word am true,
> I shall not fail that rendezvous.

More parents and children arrived. One stout man who was warming his behind at the fire, said, 'I always think those words of Asquith's after the armistice were so apt . . .'

They brought the cake close to my high chair for me to see, with the candle shining and flickering above the pink icing. 'A pity she never smiles.'

'She'll smile in time,' my mother said, obviously upset.

'What Asquith told the House of Commons just after the war,' said that stout gentleman with his backside to the fire, '– so apt, what Asquith said. He said that the war has cleansed and purged the world, by God! I recall his actual words: "All things have become new. In this great cleansing and purging it has been the privilege of our country to play her part . . ."'

That did it. I broke into a decided smile and everyone noticed it, convinced that it was provoked by the fact that my brother had blown out the candle on the cake. 'She smiled!' my mother exclaimed. And everyone was clucking away about how I was smiling. For good measure I crowed like a demented raven. 'My baby's smiling!' said my mother.

'It was the candle on her cake,' they said.

The cake be damned. Since that time I have grown to smile quite naturally, like any other healthy and house-trained person, but when I really mean a smile, deeply felt from the core, then to all intents and purposes it comes in response to the words uttered in the House of Commons after the First World War by the distinguished, the immaculately dressed and the late Mr Asquith.

The Fortune-Teller

The château lay among woodlands in a wide valley in the heart of the old Troubadour country of France. It was about ten years ago at the end of summer.

We were a party of three, Raymond, his wife Sylvia, and me, Lucy. The marriage between Raymond and Sylvia was already going bad, which made me very uncomfortable. I had already decided after the third day of our travels that I would never again go on holiday alone with a married couple, and I never have since.

I had begun to wonder why they had asked me to join them and I fairly guessed that they were trying to prove, by the evidence of my single state, that they were truly a couple. We arrived at the château after a week in France, by which time I was on the point of getting on a train to the nearest airport and so back to London.

But I changed my mind precisely at the château. Sylvia asked for rooms. Mme Dessain, thin, tall, work-worn and elegant, who had come round the side of the house with a bucket of pigswill in her hand to greet us, declined to answer Sylvia. She addressed me, saying very politely that yes, she had a double room for me and my husband and a small room for Mlle on the maids' floor at the top of the house. Raymond intervened to explain the relationships aright. She gave the sort of smile by which it was plain she had understood perfectly well. I supposed that Sylvia, who spoke French better than I did, had nevertheless lacked the required respect; she had taken Mme Dessain for one of the hired hands, and had selected her tone accordingly. This was a habit of Sylvia's; I always marvelled at the trouble she must have put into harbouring such a range of initial attitudes as she had for different people, when one alone would serve for all. She was, of course, a follower of Lenin who was class-conscious by profession. Raymond was fairly neutral about the incident. He was big and bearded, a television producer; and he was intelligent. But he was vain enough, and perhaps sufficiently at the point of exasperation with his marriage to show himself pleased with the proprietor's mistake, if mistake it was. Madame did not apologize; she merely told us the price of the rooms and asked if we wanted demi-pension. Sylvia, when angry, had a leer. Her teeth protruded and for some reason she dyed her hair bright red. In spite of this she had a handsome look. But, leering, she looked, to me, morally low, very low, and stupid although in fact she was a rodent-biologist of some distinction.

Mme Dessain put down the bucket and again addressed me. She asked me if I would like to see the rooms. Plainly, she was not too grand to be catty and she had taken against Sylvia.

'Have we decided to stay?' Sylvia said to Raymond. 'Do you like the place?'

'It looks lovely,' he said, 'I would like to see the room anyway, because I would like to stay.'

Mme Dessain led the way upstairs. I followed with my two clever friends behind me. The rooms were fine and we all decided to stay. Strangely enough I wasn't put in a maid's room upstairs, but in a large room on the same floor as my friends. Madame – it turned out that she was in fact a marquise – ran down to get on with her jobs, leaving us to cope with our luggage. I thought she looked well over fifty when I had first seen her but watching her trip so easily downstairs I could see she was younger, not much over forty. She had obviously taken a dislike to Sylvia, but I didn't care. Already I felt free of the embarrassing couple. In a curious way Mme Dessain had released me. She had held out a straw. I clutched it and miraculously it held me up. It struck me she was highly intuitive, as indeed are so many in the hotel business.

I was delighted with my room. It had windows on two sides. The furniture was French Provincial, plainly belonging to the eighteenth-century château and by no means brought in for hotel guests. It was much the same all over the house. There were two drawing-rooms, the yellow one and the green, and these were by no means rustic, but in the great high style of eighteenth-century France. There was an Oriental room with a Chinese part and an Egyptian part, full of those furnishings and treasures brought back from the travels of nineteenth century ancestors, which are too good for the use of ordinary tourists yet not too rare for everyday accommodation. It was a satisfaction to feel we had been taken in as guests, since plainly Mme Dessain had to be discriminate.

Few of the guests used the Oriental room, or the other priceless-seeming rooms with their Sèvres ornaments and plates behind glass cabinets. There was a more serviceable library in general use, with a television set, tables, and plenty of worn, cretonne-covered sofas and chairs.

It was there that a few evenings later I offered to tell Mme Dessain's fortune by cards. People were grouped around, after dinner, some just talking, others playing various card games and a couple in a far corner were playing chess. Outside it was pelting with heavy thick rain; it had been raining all day. A small, stout, elderly man was Mme Dessain's husband; a surprising couple. He sat by her side while I told her fortune. Sylvia and Raymond, bored with my fortune-telling, had moved away.

I must explain that when I find myself in a country or seaside establishment of the residential sort on any of my many travels, if I see someone lonely or ill at ease, and obviously not enjoying their stay, I always offer to tell their fortune by my cards. I've never been refused. On the contrary, it tends to have a hypnotic effect on the other guests, and candidates for my fortune-telling are never wanting; they even come up to me and ask me what I charge, and when I explain that I do it for free, they are slightly embarrassed, but want their fortune just the same, and politely accept being put off when I've had too much or for some good reason don't want to do it.

My peculiar method of fortune-telling follows no tradition of occult sciences; I follow rules, but they are my own secret ones, varying quite a lot in their application to each individual. They are my own secret rules but they arise from deep conviction. They cannot be formulated, they are as sincere and indescribable as are the primary colours; they are not of a science but of an art. Very often I make a mistake, but I know it; at such moments I'm thinking my way, talking through a dense fog, shining the torch of my intuition here and there until it hits on some object which may or may not prove to be what I say it is. Sometimes my predictions are wildly astray as they pertain to the present time and environment, but I have known them to become surprisingly true much later in life, in a different place, and presume that this may happen, too, in some of the cases where I lose sight of the person whose fortune I have told.

For the actual selection of the cards I have a precise system. I should never reveal it in detail, except to say that it is based on sevens and fives. Sevens and fives; and if you should ask me any more about this initial stage of the proceedings I should tell you a falsehood; indeed the whole of the process is most precious-fragile to me, and I wouldn't give it away lest I should lose my powers. I mean what Yeats meant:

> I have spread my dreams under your feet;
> Tread softly because you tread on my dreams.

To tell the cards I begin by asking my client to shuffle them. Then I deal according to my seven and five system; a varying number of cards which emerge from this process are set apart and I ask my client to shuffle again. Again I deal and set apart, and a third time, three cycles in all. The client then shuffles the cards which have been set aside; these are the cards of his fortune. At the same time the client is asked to make a silent wish, and mightily concentrate upon it.

Now, I take these cards and again deal them. You mustn't think that because I take my gifts seriously, I take them solemnly. It is all an airy dream of mine, unsinkable because it is light. I don't play the eerie fortune-teller at all; I don't play anything when I tell the cards; I am simply myself.

Well, I take the cards that have fallen to my client's lot and deal them under the following headings: (1) the secret self; (2) the known self (by which I mean, the more limited aspect of the person as he is observable by others); (3) the client's hopes; (4) the client's degree of self-ignorance; (5) his present destination (I don't say his 'destiny' for this reason, that any destiny I might take from the cards would be prematurely conceived and would fail to allow for a client's probable divergence from his present destination. Circumstances change. There can be a change of heart. Human nature is essentially unpredictable in the long run. But 'destination' none the less often answers for destiny. No clairvoyant, believe me, can say more); (6) affairs of the heart, which means the prevailing love; that is, of any object, including, from time to time, that of money; (7) the wish – will it or won't it come true?

Again I see Mme Dessain in the friendly library of her house leaning over the table, those many years ago, with her husband by her side as I began to tell her cards.

While she was shuffling I saw that she was extremely punctilious about the performance. While I dealt and discarded according to my secret method she watched me with an intensity that meant, to me, a decided confidence in my powers. Her wish was evidently of critical importance. She seemed absorbed by the cards that fell to constitute her fortune, but I advised her light-heartedly not to give weight to them herself, to concentrate hard on the wish, and to leave the interpretation in due time to me.

'There are many spades,' observed Mme Dessain. 'And there is an ace of spades, Madame.' I was puzzled as to why she insisted on addressing me as 'Madame' when I was plainly 'Mademoiselle'. I was dealing the third cycle. In my conjuring out of the meaning of cards I never go by the tradition. It is true that no one is delighted by the ace of spades but it does not necessarily mean a personal death. It might mean the death of a hope, or the end of a fear. Everything depends on the combination. Anyway, I was dealing the third cycle. I said, 'Leave it to me,' and finished.

Now I gathered up Mme Dessain's cards.

'Will the rain never stop?' said Mme Dessain, her eyes wandering to the enormous french windows. She was putting this on, this absent air as if she didn't care in the least about her fortune.

'Concentrate on your wish, Madame,' I said.

'Oh, I am concentrating. The rain is a tourist attraction if they like the flooded fields, very beautiful.' So she laughed off her fortune-telling, but I could see she was eager, even a little agitated. Her husband, too, watched with care. I wanted to remind them it was only a game, but I refrained; I didn't want to bring their nervousness to light.

I dealt the cards under their seven headings, which naturally I didn't pronounce. Thirteen cards had emerged from the process of selection. I noticed the high proportion of court cards in Mme Dessain's set.

Now, in the first round to her secret self, came up the eight of spades, to her known self the six of spades.

'Spades in my wish!' said Mme Dessain immediately.

'Have patience,' I said, still setting forth the cards. It was obvious to me now that she was trying to penetrate my method for when I put down the king of hearts she said, 'a fair, handsome lover.' But I gave no sign, although I felt annoyed at the interruption.

Her cards finally came out as follows:

Secret self: eight of spades and six of clubs
Known self: six of spades and nine of diamonds
Things hoped for: king of hearts and ace of spades
Self-ignorance: five of hearts and king of clubs
Present destination: queen of hearts and three of hearts
Affairs of the heart: queen of clubs and three of diamonds
The wish: knave of hearts.

Mme Dessain was really perplexed. She saw all seven sets of cards placed out before her, but she had no way of guessing the private headings I had placed them under. Her eyes were bright upon the cards as if she were telling my fortune, not me hers.

'You have got your wish,' I said at once, seeing that she had come in for one card only, the knave of hearts, under that heading, and there was no opposition. 'However, it is a wish that you should not have made.'

'Which cards represent my wish?' she asked, almost in a panic, strange for such a grand lady.

I wouldn't tell her. I smiled at her and said, 'This is only a game, after all.'

She put on an air that she was pacified, pulled together. But I could see that she was not.

Altogether, from this moment what her cards told me was one thing and what I told her was another. I had reason to be cautious. As I looked at the whole picture that was formed by the seven groups of cards it was at first a coloured mass, changing into a tableau of patterns until one idea protruded larger and more brilliantly than the others. And so, it appeared to me all in a quick moment that Mme Dessain was herself a natural clairvoyant; she was able to read my mind perhaps better than I was able to read her cards. What had been to me a laughing matter, a game, seemed now to veer rather dangerously towards myself, and I knew that her wish had been in some way connected with me. I say connected with me, not directed at me, because there was something indirect about it; at the same time it was distinctly malevolent.

I braved out the performance. I told her a certain amount of nonsense, but as I spoke I could see she discerned that I wasn't as frank as I might have been. More specifically than before I could now see under the heading of the secret self that she was clairvoyant.

Now, for instance, I looked at the known self in a special way. I felt that her very attractive, haggard and aristocratic appeal was by no means as artless as it had seemed when she was working around the outhouses or busy with the vast baronial pans in the great stone kitchen. She looked airily up at the beautiful windows, now, those tall windows with leaded corners. I was aware of her husband's attention upon her and thought he seemed jealous, wondering what had been her wish and looking for her reaction to everything I said.

I continued to say many sweet things with a grain of what seemed probable. 'You are hoping,' I said, 'for a visit from a tall bearded man, I should imagine an Englishman, who has an interest in gardening –' Indeed I received from Mme Dessain's cards a very strong premonition concerning the garden.

'That's Camillo, our odd-job man,' said the anxious husband. 'He's been away for five days, and he's overdue. But he's Italian.'

'Alain!' rebuked Mme Dessain. 'Let Mme Lucy continue.'

I continued. It did seem to me very plainly that Mme Dessain had set her heart on a visitor. He would be about her age, probably an American or an Englishman (he could have been a German but for the fact it was extremely unlikely that a woman of Mme Dessain's age and ethos would have a German lover). She was, however, moving towards this love affair full tilt. I was sure he had been a guest at the château, certainly married then, if not now, and decidedly rich. It was a disastrous enough attachment for her house and family.

All this I saw, and Mme Dessain knew that I saw it. What she was unaware of, or was bound by her infatuation to ignore, was the vast amount of bother and anxiety this course was leading her to. Her husband, though not in the least faithful to her, would make nothing but bitterness of the affair.

'You may be unaware that certain benefits will come to the house as a result of your visitor's appearance,' I said. And I told her the visitor would be poor, and warned her against unforeseen expenditure. The husband rejoiced to hear these words, and I wound up, 'Tomorrow you will receive a very important family letter,' – one of the few honest comments on Mme Dessain's cards that I chose to make. Indeed, I thought it was harmless, for the husband said, 'That will be from our son, Charles,' and Mme Dessain once more cried out, 'Alain! You interrupt.'

I said, 'I've finished.'

Mme Dessain was looking beyond me. 'Here comes Madame's husband,' she said ambiguously; anyway, I looked round and saw Raymond approaching. I guessed he had quarrelled with Sylvia who, leaving the room, looked round smiling with that deplorable angry leer of hers, which quite ruined her appearance.

I left next day. The tense atmosphere between my married friends was not to be borne by me. When I went to pay my bill Mme Dessain sent a maid to take the money and with the message that she was occupied.

But Raymond came running after me as my luggage went into the taxi. His face was fairly frantic. It struck me that he would have been rather handsome without his beard.

'Lucy,' he said. 'Lucy.'

'I'm sorry, Raymond. But I have to go.'

He was really inarticulate and I thought it quite civil of him to feel for me and my embarrassment at being on the scene of a messed-up marriage.

'Lucy.'

'My apologies to Sylvia,' I said. 'She'll understand.'

That was the last I saw of Raymond, watching my taxi depart, as he did.

Everything but the physical memory of the lovely château went far away to the back of my mind in the general nuisance of changing my holiday plans. The next week I returned to London and took up my life. Mme Dessain and the telling of her cards slept latent for year after year, but with each detail regularly arranged in case it should ever be needed, as is the way with memory.

Some time over the following year I heard that Sylvia and Raymond had finally separated; I was told that Sylvia was married again, to a social worker much younger than herself, and that after the divorce Raymond had given up his good job and gone to live abroad. Abroad is a big place and the rumours were equally too large and amorphous for me to take any account of, so busy with my own life as I was. When occasionally I thought of that holiday I shared with them I thought of the beautiful château, but a cloud came over my thoughts when I remembered how uncomfortable I felt as the third party. I didn't know till much later that they stayed on at the château for another week.

Not long ago I came across M. Dessain. I didn't recognize him at first. I was aware only of a little wizened man walking out of the Black Forest at Baden-Baden. I should say that it isn't unusual for anything whatsoever to walk out of the Black Forest, so I took no particular notice. Moreover he was dressed in beige, and I might say that every visitor to Baden-Baden wears beige, both men and women. Their clothes and their shoes are beige and their faces are beige; in which respect they are quite lovable.

But I noticed him again that day seated alone at a lunch table in the dining room of my hotel. Even then, I failed to see anything familiar about him; I only noticed that he looked at me once or twice, briefly, but in a decidedly curious way.

That evening I was sitting in the public room of the hotel playing with my cards. I was alone, waiting for a friend to join me there the next day. I shuffled my cards and dealt them out in my own style which seems so haphazard; I don't ever tell my own fortune, but I can't keep away from the cards. I shuffle and deal and see what comes up, and in the meantime my ideas take form as if the cards were a sort of sacrament, 'an outward and visible sign of an inward and spiritual grace,' as the traditional definition goes.

Up to me at my table came the wizened guest, him of the Black Forest. He sat down on the edge of a sofa, watching me. I felt he was sad, and I was about to ask him if he would like me to tell his fortune.

'Mlle Lucy,' he said.

Then I recognized him, the once chubby little husband of Mme Dessain, and I saw how the years had withered him. In all its formal detail of ten years ago or more, I remembered the features of the room in the château where I told Mme Dessain's fortune while she, intense and distressed, perceived in her clairvoyance all that I was about. I remembered the two chess players sitting quietly apart, the tall shapes of Sylvia and Raymond moving away impatiently from the scene, the worn floral fabric on the chairs. I wondered if Mme

Dessain's lover had materialized, and I recalled vaguely some of my light-hearted predictions which hadn't fooled Mme Dessain one bit. 'You are hoping for a visit from a tall, bearded Englishman, interested in the garden.' And my own sincere prediction, 'You will have a family letter.'

I looked at M. Dessain and said, 'What a long time ago. Are you on holiday?'

'I am here for my health.'

'How is Mme Dessain?' I said.

'She does very well. As you predicted, the letter came next day.'

'Oh, dear. I hope it was a good letter.'

'Yes. It came from her cousin Claude. It announced his engagement. I was delighted, because Claude was my wife's lover.'

'Oh,' I said. 'Well, that must have solved a problem for you, M. Dessain.'

'It was a good thing for Claude,' he said. 'And a good thing for you, Mlle Lucy.'

'For me?'

'My wife changed your destiny,' said the sad and withered man. He repeated, 'Your destiny, Mlle Lucy. She saw that you were destined to marry your friend Raymond, and she intervened.'

'Marry Raymond? I never thought of such a thing. There was nothing at all between us. He was on bad terms with his wife but that had nothing to do with me.'

'Nevertheless, my wife foresaw the outcome. You would have married Raymond, but after your departure, before the week was out she had him for her new lover. He is still at the château. She forestalled your destiny.'

'Not my destiny, then,' I said, 'only my destination.' And seeing that he looked so sad and so beige, I asked, 'Would you like me to tell your fortune, M. Dessain?'

He didn't answer the question. He only said, 'Raymond is very good in the garden and in the grounds.'

Christmas Fugue

As a growing schoolgirl Cynthia had been a nature-lover; in those days she had thought of herself in those terms. She would love to go for solitary walks beside a river, feel the rain on her face, lean over old walls, gazing into dark pools. She was dreamy, wrote nature-poetry. It was part of a Home Counties culture of the 1970s, and she had left all but the memories behind her when she left England to join her cousin Moira, a girl slightly older than herself, in Sydney, where Moira ran a random boutique of youthful clothes, handbags, hand-made slippers, ceramics, cushions, decorated writing paper, and many other art-like objects. Moira married a successful lawyer and moved to Adelaide. Beautiful Sydney suddenly became empty for Cynthia. She had a boyfriend. He, too, suddenly became empty. At twenty-four she wanted a new life. She had never really known the old life.

So many friends had invited her to spend Christmas Day with them that she couldn't remember how many Kind faces, smiling, 'You'll be lonely without Moira . . . What are your plans for Christmas?' Georgie (her so-called boyfriend): 'Look, you must come to us. We'd love you to come to us for Christmas. My kid brother and sister . . .'

Cynthia felt terribly empty, 'Actually, I'm going back to England.' 'So soon? Before Christmas?'

She packed her things, gave away all the stuff she didn't want. She had a one-way air ticket, Sydney–London, precisely on Christmas Day. She would spend Christmas Day on the plane. She thought all the time of all the beauty and blossoming lifestyle she was leaving behind her, the sea, the beaches, the shops, the mountains, but now it was like leaning over an old wall, dreaming. England was her destination, and really her destiny. She had never had a full adult life in England. Georgie saw her off on the plane. He was going for a new life, too, to the blue hills and wonderful colours of Brisbane, where his only uncle needed him on his Queensland sheep farm. For someone else, Cynthia thought, he won't be empty. Far from it. But he is empty for me.

She would not be alone in England. Her parents, divorced, were in their early fifties. Her brother, still unmarried, was a City accountant. An aunt had died recently; Cynthia was the executor of her will. She would not be alone in England, or in any way wondering what to do.

The plane was practically empty.

'Nobody flies on Christmas Day,' said the hostess who served the preliminary drinks. 'At least, very few. The rush is always before Christmas, and then there's always a full flight after Boxing Day till New Year when things begin to normalize.' She was talking to a young man who had remarked on the number of empty seats. 'I'm spending Christmas on the plane because I'd nowhere else to go. I thought it might be amusing.'

'It will be amusing,' said the pretty hostess. 'We'll make it fun.'

The young man looked pleased. He was a few seats in front of Cynthia. He looked around, saw Cynthia and smiled. In the course of the next hour he made it known to this small world in the air that he was a teacher returning from an exchange programme.

The plane had left Sydney at after three in the afternoon of Christmas Day. There remained over nine hours to Bangkok, their refuelling stop.

Luxuriously occupying two vacant front seats of the compartment was a middle-aged couple fully intent on their reading: he, a copy of *Time*; she, a tattered paperback of Agatha Christie's: *The Mysterious Affair at Styles*.

A thin, tall man with glasses passed the couple on the way to the lavatories. On his emergence he stopped, pointed at the paperback and said, 'Agatha Christie! You're reading Agatha Christie. She's a serial killer. On your dark side you yourself are a serial killer.' The man beamed triumphantly and made his way to a seat behind the couple.

A steward appeared and was called by the couple, both together. 'Who's that man?' – 'Did you hear what he said? He said I am a serial killer.'

'Excuse me, sir, is there something wrong?' the steward demanded of the man with glasses.

'Just making an observation,' the man replied.

The steward disappeared into the front of the plane, and reappeared with a uniformed officer, a co-pilot, who had in his hand a sheet of paper, evidently a list of passengers. He glanced at the seat number of the bespectacled offender, then at him: 'Professor Sygmund Schatt?'

'Sygmund spelt with a y,' precised the professor.

'Nothing wrong. I was merely making a professional observation.'

'Keep them to yourself in future.'

'I will not be silenced,' said Sygmund Schatt. 'Plot and scheme against me as you may.'

The co-pilot went to the couple, bent towards them, and whispered something reassuring.

'You see!' said Schatt.

The pilot walked up the aisle towards Cynthia. He sat down beside her.

'A complete nut. They do cause anxiety on planes. But maybe he's harmless. He'd better be. Are you feeling lonely?'

Cynthia looked at the officer. He was good-looking, fairly young, young enough. 'Just a bit,' she said.

'First class is empty,' said the officer. 'Like to come there?'

'I don't want to –'

'Come with me,' he said. 'What's your name?'

'Cynthia. What's yours?'

'Tom. I'm one of the pilots. There are three of us today so far. Another's coming on at Bangkok.'

'That makes me feel safe.'

It fell about that at Bangkok, when everyone else had got off the plane to stretch their legs for an hour and a half; the passengers had gone to walk around the departments of the Duty Free shop, buy presents 'from Bangkok' of a useless nature such as dolls and silk ties, to drink coffee and other beverages with biscuits and pastries; Tom and Cynthia stayed on. They made love in a beautifully appointed cabin with real curtains in the

windows – unrealistic yellow flowers on a white background. Then they talked about each other, and made
love again.

'Christmas Day,' he said. 'I'll never forget this one.'

'Nor me,' she said.

They had half an hour before the crew and passengers would rejoin them. One of the tankers which had
refuelled the plane could be seen moving off.

Cynthia luxuriated in the washroom with its toilet
waters and toothbrushes. She made herself fresh and
pretty, combed her well-cut casque of dark hair. When
she got back to the cabin he was returning from some-
where, looking young, smiling. He gave her a box.
'Christmas present.'

It contained a set of plaster Christmas crib figures,
'made in China'. A kneeling Virgin and St Joseph, the
baby Jesus and a shoemaker with his bench, a wood-
cutter, an unidentifiable monk, two shepherds and two
angels.

Cynthia arranged them on the table in front of her.

'Do you believe in it?' she said.

'Well, I believe in Christmas.'

'Yes, I, too. It means a new life. I don't see any mother
and father really kneeling beside the baby's cot worship-
ping it, do you?'

'No, that part's symbolic.'

'These are simply lovely,' she said touching her presents. 'Made of real stuff, not plastic.'

'Let's celebrate,' he said. He disappeared and returned with a bottle of champagne.

'How expensive . . .'

'Don't worry. It flows on First.'

'Will you be going on duty?'

'No,' he said. 'I clock in tomorrow.'

They made love again, high up in the air.

After that, Cynthia walked back to her former compartment. Professor Sygmund Schatt was having an argument with a hostess about his food which had apparently been pre-ordered, and now, in some way, did not come up to scratch. Cynthia sat in her old seat and, taking a postcard from the pocket in front of her, wrote to her cousin Moira. 'Having a lovely time at 35,000 feet. I have started a new life. Love XX Cynthia.' She then felt this former seat was part of the old life, and went back again to first.

In the night Tom came and sat beside her.

'You didn't eat much,' he said.

'How did you know?'

'I noticed.'

'I didn't feel up to the Christmas dinner,' she said.

'Would you like something now?'

'A turkey sandwich. Let me go and ask the hostess.'

'Leave it to me.'

Tom told her he was now in the final stages of a divorce. His wife had no doubt had a hard time of it, his job taking him away so much. But she could have studied something. She wouldn't learn, hated to learn.

And he was lonely. He asked her to marry him, and she wasn't in the least surprised. But she said, 'Oh, Tom, you don't know me.'

'I think I do.'

'We don't know each other.'

'Well, I think we should do.'

She said she would think about it. She said she would cancel her plans and come to spend some time in his flat in London at Camden Town.

'I'll have my time off within three days – by the end of the week,' he said.

'God, is he all right, is he reliable?' she said to herself. 'Am I safe with him? Who is he?' But she was really carried away.

Around four in the morning she woke and found him beside her. He said, 'It's Boxing Day now. You're a lovely girl.'

She had always imagined she was, but had always, so far, fallen timid when with men. She had experienced two brief love affairs in Australia, neither memorable. All alone in the first-class compartment with Tom, high in the air – this was reality, something to be remembered, the start of a new life.

'I'll give you the key of the flat,' he said. 'Go straight there. Nobody will disturb you. I've been sharing it with my young brother. But he's away for about six weeks I should say. In fact he's doing time. He got mixed up in a football row and he's in for grievous bodily harm and affray. Only, the bodily harm wasn't so grievous. He was just in the wrong place at the wrong time. Anyway, the flat's free for at least six weeks.'

At the airport, despite the early hour of ten past five in the morning, there was quite a crowd to meet the plane. Having retrieved her luggage, Cynthia pushed her trolley towards the exit. She had no expectation whatsoever that anyone would be there to meet her.

Instead, there was her father and his wife, Elaine;
there was her mother with her husband Bill; crowding
behind them at the barrier were her brother and his
girlfriend, her cousin Moira's cousin by marriage, and
a few other men and women whom she did not iden-
tify, accompanied, too, by some children of about ten
to fourteen. In fact her whole family, known and
unknown, had turned out to meet Cynthia. How had
they known the hour of her arrival? She had promised,
only to ring them when she got to England. 'Your cousin
Moira,' said her father, 'told us your flight. We wanted
you home, you know that.'

She went first to her mother's house. It was now
Boxing Day but they had saved Christmas Day for her
arrival. All the Christmas rituals were fully observed.
The tree and the presents – dozens of presents for
Cynthia. Her brother and his girl with some other
cousins came over for Christmas dinner.

When they came to open the presents, Cynthia
brought out from her luggage a number of packages
she had brought from Australia for the occasion. Among
them, labelled for her brother, was a plaster Nativity
set, made in China.

'What a nice one,' said her brother. 'One of the best
I've ever seen, and not plastic.'

'I got it in Moira's boutique,' Cynthia said. 'She has
very special things.'

She talked a lot about Australia, its marvels. Then,
at tea-time, they got down to her aunt's will, of which
Cynthia was an executor. Cynthia felt happy, in her
element, as an executor to a will, for she was normally
dreamy, not legally minded at all and now she felt the

flattery of her aunt's confidence in her. The executor-ship gave her some sort of authority in the family. She was now arranging, too, to spend New Year with her father and his second clan.

Her brother had set out the Nativity figures on a table. 'I don't know,' she said, 'why the mother and the father are kneeling beside the child; it seems so unreal.' She didn't hear what the others said, if anything, in response to this observation. She only felt a strange stir-ring of memory. There was to be a flat in Camden Town, but she had no idea of the address.

'The plane stopped at Bangkok,' she told them.

'Did you get off?'

'Yes, but you know you can't get out of the airport. There was a coffee bar and a lovely shop.'

It was later that day, when she was alone, unpack-ing, in her room, that she rang the airline.

'No,' said a girl's voice, 'I don't think there are curtains with yellow flowers in the first-class cabins. I'll have to ask. Was there any particular reason . . . ?'

'There was a co-pilot called Tom. Can you give me his full name please? I have an urgent message for him.'

'What flight did you say?'

Cynthia told her not only the flight but her name and original seat number in Business Class.

After a long wait, the voice spoke again, 'Yes, you are one of the arrivals.'

'I know that,' said Cynthia.

'I can't give you information about our pilots, I'm afraid. But there was no pilot on the plane called Tom . . . Thomas, no. The stewards in Business were Bob, Andrew, Sheila and Lilian.'

'No pilot called Tom? About thirty-five, tall, brown hair. I met him. He lives in Camden Town.' Cynthia gripped the phone. She looked round at the reality of the room.

'The pilots are Australian; I can tell you that but no more. I'm sorry. They're our personnel.'

'It was a memorable flight. Christmas Day. I'll never forget that one,' said Cynthia.

'Thank you. We appreciate that,' said the voice. It seemed thousands of miles away.

The Executor

When my uncle died all the literary manuscripts went
to a university foundation, except one. The correspondence went too, and the whole of his library. They came
(a white-haired man and a young girl) and surveyed his
study. Everything, they said, would be desirable and it
would make a good price if I let the whole room go –
his chair, his desk, the carpet, even his ashtrays. I agreed
to this. I left everything in the drawers of the desk just
as it was when my uncle died, including the bottle of
Librium and a rusty razor blade.

My uncle died this way: he was sitting on the bank of
the river, playing a fish. As the afternoon faded a man
passed by, and then a young couple who made pottery
passed him. As they said later, he was sitting peacefully
awaiting the catch and of course they didn't disturb him.
As night fell the colonel and his wife passed by; they were
on their way home from their daily walk. They knew it
was too late for my uncle to be simply sitting there, so
they went to look. He had been dead, the doctor
pronounced, from two to two and a half hours. The fish
was still struggling with the bait. It was a mild heart
attack. Everything my uncle did was mild, so different
from everything he wrote. Yet perhaps not so different.
He was supposed to be 'far out', so one didn't know what
went on out there. Besides, he had not long returned
from a trip to London. They say, still waters run deep.

But far out was how he saw himself. He once said that if you could imagine modern literature as a painting, perhaps by Brueghel the Elder, the people and the action were in the foreground, full of colour, eating, stealing, copulating, laughing, courting each other, excreting, and stabbing each other, selling things, climbing trees. Then in the distance, at the far end of a vast plain, there he would be, a speck on the horizon, always receding and always there, and always a necessary and mysterious component of the picture; always there and never to be taken away, essential to the picture – a speck in the distance, which if you were to blow up the detail would simply be a vague figure, plodding on the other way.

I am no fool, and he knew it. He didn't know it at first, but he had seven months in which to learn that fact. I gave up my job in Edinburgh in the government office, a job with a pension, to come here to the lonely house among the Pentland Hills to live with him and take care of things. I think he imagined I was going to be another Elaine when he suggested the arrangement. He had no idea how much better I was for him than Elaine. Elaine was his mistress, that is the stark truth. 'My common-law wife,' he called her, explaining that in Scotland, by tradition, the woman you are living with is your wife. As if I didn't know all that nineteenth-century folklore; and it's long died out. Nowadays you have to do more than say 'I marry you, I marry you, I marry you,' to make a woman your wife. Of course, my uncle was a genius and a character. I allowed for that. Anyway, Elaine died and I came here a month later. Within a month I had cleared up the best part of the disorder. He called me a Scottish puritan girl, and at forty-one it was nice to be a girl and I wasn't against the Scottish puritanical attribution either since I am proud to be a Scot; I feel nationalistic about it. He always had that smile of his when he said it, so I don't know how he meant it. They say he had that smile of his when he was found dead, fishing.

'I appoint my niece Susan Kyle to be my sole literary executor.' I don't wonder he decided on this course after I had been with him for three months. Probably for the first time in his life all his papers were in order. I went into Edinburgh and bought box-files and cover-files and I filed away all that mountain of papers, each under its separate heading. And I knew what was what. You didn't catch me filing away a letter from Angus Wilson or Saul Bellow in the same place as an ordinary 'W' or 'B', a Miss Mary Whitelaw or a Mrs Jonathan Brown. I knew the value of these letters, they went into a famous-persons file, bulging and of value. So that in a short time my uncle said, 'There's little for me to do now, Susan, but die.' Which I thought was melodramatic, and said so. But I could see he was forced to admire my good sense. He said, 'You remind me of my mother, who prepared her shroud all ready for her funeral.' His mother was my grandmother Janet Kyle. Why shouldn't she have sat and sewn her shroud? People in those days had very little to do, and here I was running the house and looking after my uncle's papers with only the help of Mrs Donaldson three mornings a week, where my grandmother had four pairs of hands for indoor help and three out. The rest of the family never went near the house after my grandmother died, for Elaine was always there with my uncle.

The property was distributed among the family, but I was the sole literary executor. And it was up to me to do what I liked with his literary remains. It was a good thing I had everything inventoried and filed, ready for sale. They came and took the total archive as they called it away, all the correspondence and manuscripts except one. That one I kept for myself. It was the novel he was writing when he died, an unfinished manuscript. I thought, Why not? Maybe I will finish it myself and publish it. I am no fool, and my uncle must have known how the book was going to end. I never read any of his correspondence, mind you; I was too busy those months filing it all in order. I did think, however, that I would read this manuscript and perhaps put an ending to it. There were already ten chapters. My uncle had told me there was only another chapter to go. So I said nothing to the Foundation about that one unfinished manuscript; I was only too glad when they had come and gone, and the papers were out of the house. I got the painters in to clean the study. Mrs Donaldson said she had never seen the house looking so like a house should be.

Under my uncle's will I inherited the house, and I planned eventually to rent rooms to tourists in the summer, bed and breakfast. In the meantime I set about reading the unfinished manuscript, for it was only April, and I'm not a one to let the grass grow under my feet. I had learnt to decipher that old-fashioned handwriting of his which looked good on the page but was not too clear. My uncle had a treasure in me those last months of his life, although he said I was like a book without an index – all information, and no way of getting at it. I asked him to tell me what information he ever got out of Elaine, who never passed an exam in her life.

This last work of my uncle's was an unusual story for him, set in the seventeenth century here among the Pentland Hills. He had told me only that he was writing something strong and cruel, and that this was easier to accomplish in a historical novel. It was about the slow identification and final trapping of a witch, and I could see as I read it that he hadn't been joking when he said it was strong and cruel; he had often said things to frighten and alarm me, I don't know why. By chapter ten the trial of the witch in Edinburgh was only halfway through. Her fate depended entirely on chapter eleven, and on the negotiations that were being conducted behind the scenes by the opposing factions of intrigue. My uncle had left a pile of notes he had accumulated towards this novel, and I retained these along with the manuscript. But there was no sign in the notes as to how my uncle had decided to resolve the fate of the witch – whose name was Edith but that is by the way. I put the notebooks and papers away, for there were many other things to be done following the death of my famous uncle. The novel itself was written by hand in twelve notebooks. In the twelfth only the first two pages had been filled, the rest of the pages were blank; I am sure of this. The two filled pages came to the end of chapter ten. At the top of the next page was written 'Chapter Eleven'. I looked through the rest of the notebook to make sure my uncle had not made some note there on how he intended to continue; all blank, I am sure of it. I put the twelve notebooks, together with the sheaf of loose notes, in a drawer of the solid-mahogany dining-room sideboard.

A few weeks later I brought the notebooks out again, intending to consider how I might proceed with the completion of the book and so enhance its value. I read again through chapter ten; then, when I turned to the page where 'Chapter Eleven' was written, there in my uncle's handwriting was the following:

> *Well, Susan, how do you feel about finishing my novel? Aren't you a greedy little snoot, holding back my unfinished work, when you know the Foundation paid for the lot? What about your puritanical principles? Elaine and I are waiting to see how you manage to write Chapter Eleven. Elaine asks me to add it's lovely to see you scouring and cleaning those neglected corners of the house. But don't you know, Jaimie is having you on. Where does he go after lunch?*
>
> *– Your affect Uncle*

I could hardly believe my eyes. The first shock I got was the bit about Jaimie, and then came the second shock, that the words were there at all. It was twelve-thirty at night and Jaimie had gone home. Jaimie Donaldson is the son of Mrs Donaldson, and it isn't his fault he's out of work. We have had experiences together, but nobody is to know that, least of all Mrs Donaldson who introduced him into the household merely to clean the windows and stoke the boiler. But the words? Where did they come from?

It is a lonely house, here in a fold of the Pentlands, surrounded by woods, five miles to the nearest cottage, six to Mrs Donaldson's, and the buses stop at ten p.m. I felt a great fear there in the dining-room, with the twelve notebooks on the table, and the pile of papers, a great cold, and a panic. I ran to the hall and lifted the telephone but didn't know how to explain myself or whom to phone. My story would sound like that of a woman gone crazy. Mrs Donaldson? The police? I couldn't think what to say to them at that hour of night. 'I have found some words that weren't there before in my uncle's manuscript, and in his own hand.' It was unthinkable. Then I thought perhaps someone had played me a trick. Oh no, I knew that this couldn't be. Only Mrs Donaldson had been in the dining-room, and only to dust, with me to help her. Jaimie had no chance to go there, not at all. I never used the dining-room now and had meals in the kitchen. But in fact I knew it wasn't them, it was Uncle. I wished with all my heart that I was a strong woman, as I had always felt I was, strong and sensible. I stood in the hall by the telephone, shaking. 'O God, everlasting and almighty,' I prayed, 'make me strong, and guide and lead me as to how Mrs Thatcher would conduct herself in circumstances of this nature.'

I didn't sleep all night. I sat in the big kitchen stoking up the fire. Only once I moved, to go back into the dining-room and make sure that those words were there. Beyond a doubt they were, and in my uncle's handwriting – that handwriting it would take an expert forger to copy. I put the manuscript back in the drawer; I locked the dining-room door and took the key. My uncle's study, now absolutely empty, was above the kitchen. If he was haunting the house, I heard no sound from there or from anywhere else. It was a fearful night, waiting there by the fire.

Mrs Donaldson arrived in the morning, complaining that Jaimie was getting lazy; he wouldn't rise. Too many late nights.

'Where does he go after lunch?' I said.

'Oh, he goes for a round of golf after his dinner,' she said. 'He's always ready for a round of golf no matter what else there is to do. Golf is the curse of Scotland.'

I had a good idea who Jaimie was meeting on the golf course, and I could almost have been grateful to Uncle for pointing out to me in that sly way of his that Jaimie wandered in the hours after the midday meal which we called lunch and they called their dinner. By five o'clock in the afternoon Jaimie would come here to the house to fetch up the coal, bank the fire, and so forth. But all afternoon he would be on the links with that girl who works at the manse, Greta, younger sister of Elaine, the one who moved in here openly, ruining my uncle's morals, leaving the house to rot. I always suspected that family. After Elaine died it came out he had even introduced her to all his friends; I could tell from the letters of condolence, how they said things like 'He never got over the loss of Elaine' and 'He couldn't live without her'. And sometimes he called me Elaine by mistake. I was furious. Once, for example, I said, 'Uncle, stop pacing about down here. Go up to your study and do your scribbling; I'll bring you a cup of cocoa.' He said, with that glaze-eyed look he always had when he was interrupted in his thoughts, 'What's come over you, Elaine?' I said, 'I'm not Elaine, thank you very much.' 'Oh, of course,' he said, 'you are not Elaine, you are most certainly not her.' If the public that read his books by the tens of thousands could have seen behind the scenes, I often wondered what they would have

thought. I told him so many a time, but he smiled in that
sly way, that smile he still had on his face when they found
him fishing and stone dead.

After Mrs Donaldson left the house, at noon, I went
up to my bedroom, half dropping from lack of sleep.
Mrs Donaldson hadn't noticed anything, you could be
falling down dead – they never look at you. I slept till
four. It was still light. I got up and locked the doors, front
and back. I pulled the curtains shut, and when Jaimie
rang the bell at five o'clock I didn't open, I just let him
ring. Eventually he went away. I expect he had plenty to
wonder about. But I wasn't going to make him welcome
before the fire and get him his supper, and take off my
clothes there in the back room on the divan with him,
in front of the television, while Uncle and Elaine were
looking on, even though it is only Nature. No, I turned
on the television for myself. You would never believe, it
was a programme on the Scottish BBC about Uncle. I
switched to TV One, and got a quiz show. And I felt
hungry, for I'd eaten nothing since the night before.

But I couldn't face any supper until I had assured
myself about that manuscript. I was fairly certain by
now that it was a dream. 'Maybe I've been overwork-
ing,' I thought to myself. I had the key of the dining-
room in my pocket and I took it and opened the door;
I closed the curtains, and I went to the drawer and took
out the notebook.

Not only were the words that I had read last night
there, new words were added, a whole paragraph:

Look up the Acts of the Apostles, Chapter 5, verses 1 to 10.
See what happened to Ananias and Sapphira his wife.

*You're not getting on very fast with your scribbling, are you,
Susan? Elaine and I were under the impression you were
going to write Chapter Eleven. Why don't you take a cup of
cocoa and get on with it? First read Acts, V, 1–10.*

– Your affec Uncle

Well, I shoved the book in the drawer and looked round
the dining-room. I looked under the table and behind the
curtains. It didn't look as if anything had been touched.
I got out of the room and locked the door, I don't know
how. I went to fetch my Bible, praying, 'O God omnipo-
tent and all-seeing, direct and instruct me as to the way
out of this situation, astonishing as it must appear to
Thee.' I looked up the passage:

But a certain man named Ananias, with Sapphira his wife,
sold a possession.

And kept back part of the price, his wife also being privy to
it, and brought a certain part and laid it at the apostles' feet.

But Peter said, Ananias, why hath Satan filled thine heart
to lie to the Holy Ghost, and to keep back part of the land?

I didn't read any more because I knew how it went
on. Ananias and Sapphira, his wife, were both struck
dead for holding back the portion of the sale for themselves. This was Uncle getting at me for holding back
his manuscript from the Foundation. That's an impu-
dence, I thought, to make such a comparison from
the Bible, when he was an open and avowed sinner
himself.

I thought it all over for a while. Then I went into the
dining-room and got out that last notebook. Something

else had been written since I had put it away, not half an hour before:

Why don't you get on with Chapter Eleven? We're waiting for it.

I tore out the page, put the book away and locked the door. I took the page to the fire and put it on to burn. Then I went to bed.

This went on for a month. My uncle always started the page afresh with 'Chapter Eleven', followed by a new message. He even went so far as to put in that I had kept back bits of the housekeeping money, although, he wrote, I was well paid enough. That's a matter of opinion, and who did the economising, anyway? Always, after reading Uncle's disrespectful comments, I burned the page, and we were getting near the end of the notebook. He would say things to show he followed me round the house, and even knew my dreams. When I went into Edinburgh for some shopping he knew exactly where I had been and what I'd bought. He and Elaine listened in to my conversations on the telephone if I rang up an old friend. I didn't let anyone in the house except Mrs Donaldson. No more Jaimie. He even knew if I took a dose of salts and how long I had sat in the bathroom, the awful old man.

Mrs Donaldson one morning said she was leaving. She said to me, 'Why don't you see a doctor?' I said, 'Why?' But she wouldn't speak.

One day soon afterwards a man rang me up from the Foundation. They didn't want to bother me, they said, but they were rather puzzled. They had found in

Uncle's letters many references to a novel, *The Witch of the Pentlands*, which he had been writing just before his death; and they had found among the papers a final chapter to this novel, which he had evidently written on loose pages on a train, for a letter of his, kindly provided by one of his many correspondents, proved this. Only they had no idea where the rest of the manuscript could be. In the end the witch Edith is condemned to be burned, but dies of her own will power before the execution, he said, but there must be ten more chapters leading up to it. This was Uncle's most metaphysical work, and based on a true history, the man said, and he must stress that it was very important.

I said that I would have a look. I rang back that afternoon and said I had found the whole book in a drawer in the dining-room.

So the man came to get it. On the phone he sounded very suspicious, in case there were more manuscripts. 'Are you sure that's everything? You know, the Foundation's price included the whole archive. No, don't trust it to the mail, I'll be there tomorrow at two.'

Just before he arrived I took a good drink, whisky and soda, as, indeed, I had been taking from sheer need all the past month. I had brought out the notebooks. On the blank page was written:

Goodbye, Susan. It's lovely being a speck in the distance.
                              Your affec Uncle

POCKET PENGUINS

1. Lady Chatterley's Trial
2. **Eric Schlosser** Cogs in the Great Machine
3. **Nick Hornby** Otherwise Pandemonium
4. **Albert Camus** Summer in Algiers
5. **P. D. James** Innocent House
6. **Richard Dawkins** The View from Mount Improbable
7. **India Knight** On Shopping
8. **Marian Keyes** Nothing Bad Ever Happens in Tiffany's
9. **Jorge Luis Borges** The Mirror of Ink
10. **Roald Dahl** A Taste of the Unexpected
11. **Jonathan Safran Foer** The Unabridged Pocketbook of Lightning
12. **Homer** The Cave of the Cyclops
13. **Paul Theroux** Two Stars
14. **Elizabeth David** Of Pageants and Picnics
15. **Anaïs Nin** Artists and Models
16. **Antony Beevor** Christmas at Stalingrad
17. **Gustave Flaubert** The Desert and the Dancing Girls
18. **Anne Frank** The Secret Annexe
19. **James Kelman** Where I Was
20. **Hari Kunzru** Noise
21. **Simon Schama** The Bastille Falls
22. **William Trevor** The Dressmaker's Child
23. **George Orwell** In Defence of English Cooking
24. **Michael Moore** Idiot Nation
25. **Helen Dunmore** Rose, 1944
26. **J. K. Galbraith** The Economics of Innocent Fraud
27. **Gervase Phinn** The School Inspector Calls
28. **W. G. Sebald** Young Austerlitz
29. **Redmond O'Hanlon** Borneo and the Poet
30. **Ali Smith** Ali Smith's Supersonic 70s
31. **Sigmund Freud** Forgetting Things
32. **Simon Armitage** King Arthur in the East Riding
33. **Hunter S. Thompson** Happy Birthday, Jack Nicholson
34. **Vladimir Nabokov** Cloud, Castle, Lake
35. **Niall Ferguson** 1914: Why the World Went to War